The Lightning Games

www.peridodos.com

Ordering Information:
Please visit www.peridodos.com for more information.

Printed in the United States of America

KDP ISBN: 9798406713303

Let The Games Begin!

The Lightning Games

Once upon a time, long long ago, there was a little town called Thunder Valley. This valley is very difficult to find, because of the electric charges, forming a shield. A shield which makes this special place nonexistent to other human races. The world maps simply skip over this prominent valley. The kings and queens who ruled there are very strict about one very fun thing...The Lightning Games.

Once a year, all the kids from ages seven to fifteen race to be in the final game, the Lightning Horse Game. These games are always looked forward to, and always happen whenever the special thunderstorm begins. Bolts of neon yellow, green, red, blue, pink, purple and orange lightning dominate the sky. Booming claps of thunder echo through the streets and mountains.

The villagers of Thunder Valley are different from people we normally see and interact with. The villager's skin, hair, and eyes are different colors. Their skin, hair and eye color can be green, orange, yellow, pink, blue, red, and purple. Aside from that, they can be different shades of colors. For example, from an electric neon blue to a dark deep sea blue. A neon green, to a forest green. These traits are passed down from the children's parents through genetics, however color shades can be slightly different.

Elders tell legends of the royal family. Everyone knows that each member of the royal family wears clothing of only their colors. They say that each family member takes turns traveling to the highest mountain peak during the very start of the special thunderstorm. Usually three royalty get chosen to be converted into a glowing horse used in the games. The three royalty await there, while chanting an incantation over and over again. The royal family member then gets transformed by being struck by a harmless magical lightning bolt. This transfigures them into a beautiful strong horse glowing with their personal given color. They then are transported to the stone stadium, where the final game of The Lightning Games will occur.

Now you may wonder how each family member is given their color. The royalty are all born in different years, but only on the day of the special lightning storm. This lightning storm usually happens from late spring to early fall, only once a year. Now instead of going to the highest peak like being transformed into a horse, the pregnant mother of the Royal family makes her way down to the lowest peak bringing along with her a white cotton blanket.

At the top of the lowest peak, there is a comfortable stone gazebo with a hole in the center of the roof. Feather cushions are stacked by the one entrance covered with beautifully dyed cotton covers. Once she makes herself comfortable, she gives birth to her child. All the royalty's skin colors are the purest pearl white. She wraps the child with the white cotton blanket and the mother places the baby a few feet away from her. She chants an incantation once, and the baby is struck with a bolt of lightning with their personal color. The infant begins to glow brightly, matching the color of the lightning bolt. The white blanket also changes color to match the color of the glow. After a few minutes, the glow dims, but the blanket remains the same as the baby's personal color. Then the mother and child make their way back to the castle.

Now these are stories and legends. No one knows if these are actually true, but they have been passed down through generations. So many generations, that no one knows if anyone actually saw these events for themselves. Many think that the person who possibly saw these events is the reason why the people of Thunder Valley are not allowed in the mountains. Therefore, these stories are classified as true, even though no one can prove it.

The morning of the Thunderstorm, everyone wakes up to a heavily clouded valley. Any other day of the year is not the same. These clouds are very dense, and when the sun starts to shine through them, you see bright neon colors and colors that usually aren't in a regular rainbow. It is crisp and cool out, and everything is quiet and still. As people start waking up, they notice the weather. An hour after the sun has fully risen, the sky becomes darker, and the thunder starts to rumble. Soon after, the lightning starts to shoot down and out of the clouds. This is when everyone absolutely knows that the Lightning Games are going to occur. The villagers eat their breakfast, carry out their daily morning chores, and complete some extra chores so they don't have to do so many afterwards. Everyone eats an early lunch, and gathers everyone in their family to depart to the place where the games will begin.

The children race ahead of their parents, through the streets, to the stone building in the meadow. With eager faces, they line up at the starting line. Adults mingle behind a line of electric blue lightning. As soon as all the villagers are there, the old man comes out of the old gray stoned building. The roof is thatched long grass, browned from years of rain and sun. The wooden shutters are closed, but the big cracks between the wood pieces suggest that a good amount of light comes in even with them closed. The old man that came out of the building serves the royal family. He is the only person that mediates the Lightning Games. His face is covered with wrinkles, his silvery hair seems to glow with each bolt of electricity. He wears worn down baggy pants, a patched up shirt, and shoes riddled with holes. In his hand, he holds a high pitched flute. In the other, a leather cone to make his voice louder to tell us what to do.

He claps once, and a bolt of lightning strikes the ground twenty feet away from us. The light's blinding, and what it leaves behind is the obstacle course we will get through for the games. In the distance, I see the tall gray stoned stadium looming over a short white stone building. The stadium is where the final game will be held, and the white building is where a maze is.

The old man raises the cone to his mouth and everyone quiets. He clears his throat, and starts to talk. His voice is hoarse, and sounds rough, but we all understand him. He says, “Today is the day of the Lightning Games. You children will have to go through an obstacle course of Lightning bolts shooting down. If you get hit, you will be frozen there for five seconds, before being able to continue. Then you make your way through a maze and find a lightning bolt figurine while inside. There will be 5 figurines to find. Each person will have to find one to hand into the man at the sticker station in order to participate in the last games. Then you have to find your way to a sticker station, and pick out what the man says. Next, you will race to the stadium, making sure that the giant Ogre doesn’t see you. If you are noticed and seen moving, you will have to take five big steps back, or the Ogre will gladly help you with that. Once past the Ogre, the first 3 participants will participate in the Lightning Horse Game. Instructions will be given to those three players once there. This year, there will be only two horses of the usual three. The royalty wanted to change things up and make it interesting. Now, let the games begin!"

The children strike their positions at the starting line. The adults hold their breath. The group is silent. The birds and bugs are quiet in the trees and grass. The sound of thunder is extinguished. The old man, who's name is unknown, takes the flute and puts it up to his lips. He looks to the tall, noble, silent gray stone castle's balcony in the distance, where everyone knows the brightly dressed noble royalty are watching them closely.

He looks at us again, and the high pitched shriek of the flute pierces through the air. Children run through the field getting struck once every so often, while dodging the bolts of harmless lightning intended only for the game. A giant white stone building stands before them, and they enter, including us.

My sister and I are competing in the game. I am fourteen and my sister is ten. We have been competing for a while. My name is Lightning and my sister's name is Shimmer. We both have dark brown hair, orange eyes, and skin as pale as the fluffy white snow that falls and piles up in the winter. Our father has dark brown hair and bright pink eyes, and our mother has red hair and orange eyes. We all have pale white skin that people say shimmer like moonlight on the snow. In this game, my sister and I plan to stay together and win, or at least get to participate in the Lightning Horse Game.

Pathways are everywhere in this maze. We run through hallways, and take a lot of wrong turns. We meet with other kids that try to mislead us, telling us that they know where one of the figurines are. Shimmer remembers where one of the figurines were last time, so we go to the same spot. It took a while to figure out where in the maze the spot was last time. We find one of the figurines on the way after taking some lucky wrong turns, but we still have to find another. Shimmer leads me to the spot, and thankfully it was there.

After we snatched it off the ground, a group of boys came up to us from behind. They always sit at the back of the classroom at school. I recognize some of them, and know a few of their names, but some of the other boys I haven't seen before. The one that looks like the head of the group who I haven't met before, puts on a nice smile and asks us, "May we join your team?" At once,

I knew that this was a ruse for them to take our already collected figurines. Shimmer quickly answered to them, “Not this time boys, but maybe next year.” I saw the boy’s smile disappear and turn into a scowl before saying, “Give us the figurines, and we’ll let you pass. If you don’t, We’ll take them from you. You both have thirty seconds to come to an agreement of what you want to do.” Shimmer and I have already talked and practiced what we would do if this happened.

Shimmer nodded to me, and I held both of the figurines out toward him. With my arms fully extended, He reached for them, but I quickly pulled the figurines towards me, and ducked under the other stunned boys. I sprinted at full speed turning into pathways in different directions with Shimmer at my heel. The thundering footsteps and angry yells reached our ears, but we were already too far away for them to catch up and find us. I lead Shimmer back where we came from, and to the end of the maze. We luckily find a shortcut, making us the first ones to the sticker station.

It is a wooden cart filled with stickers of different colors. We handed the lightning bolt figurines over to the man standing behind the cart. The middle aged man with deep purple eyes, green hair, and red skin tells us to pick out a cinnamon colored sticker or a brightly colored sticker. I pick out a cinnamon colored one, and Shimmer quickly picks out a similar color. Two other kids reach the station before we exit out of the door leading out of the building.

A long green grass field separates us from the large stadium in front of us. In the distance, I see a giant Ogre guarding the entrance to the stadium. The Ogre has pink skin, and is dressed well. The way he is dressed with his suit and tie, hat, long pants and shiny black shoes suggests that he works closely with the royalty. He bellows, “Let the game begin!” We clearly see him turn around, and we cautiously run towards him. He starts to turn around, and we stop. The Ogre says, “I’m watching you, you better watch your step.” He sounds like he’s already having a fun time, and is playing around with us. He turns around but for a shorter time than I expected. I am caught mid stride as I stop running. “You!” The Ogre says. “Take five big steps backwards!” I take the big steps, and he nods his head in approval.

I am behind Shimmer now, and she looks back at me. I motion for her to look ahead, and continue, and she complies. The ogre turns around, and this time I’m more careful. This happens a few more times, before I hear shouts and laughter behind us. I glance around, and see a group of three kids at the exit of the white stoned building we came from.

They are taller than us, and I can tell that they're friends. "Come and get us Ogre!" One of them said. All three of them start running towards us. Shimmer and I are halfway across the field, and the group is already a quarter across. "Stop you children!" The Ogre roars. I look at him, and he doesn't look happy at all. He stands his ground though, and soon the group runs past us. The ogre is still watching us, and the others, so we can't move.

The group gets closer and closer to the Ogre, until they stop directly in front of him. "Let us pass!" a girl shrieks at the Ogre. He growls in fury, and says, "No! You must play my game correctly in order to pass through this archway. Now run back to the door in the white building." None of the three kids moved. The Ogre says again with anger still in his voice, “What are you waiting for? Get a move on, or I will remove you from the game.” With that, one of the girls steps back and starts running towards us, and to the other building.

We watch the others still unmoved in front of the Ogre. “Very well then! I will remove you from the game.” The Ogre says. In one swift motion, he grabs both of the kids, and marches a few steps along the wall. Shimmer and I take a few steps forward. Then one by one, he hangs them by the collar on hooks. They kick around, and the Ogre stands in front of them. “Let us down please.” One of them pleaded. The Ogre responds, “Only if you promise to sit here and watch the remainder of my games. If you do not, you will remain on the hooks for the rest of the games, although I will allow you to watch the games inside the stadium. Is that understood?” The kids nod, and the Ogre lifts them up and puts them on the grass. They sit down, facing the field.

The Ogre returns to the entrance of the stadium, and is pleased to see us still there. More kids arrive at the starting line next to the girl. The Ogre turns around, and we run closer. We stop as the Ogre turns back to face us, and a few turns later, a few kids are caught. The game continues, with more stops for children to take steps backwards. The game is fun, even though we both have to take some steps back. We reach the Ogre too soon, even though we want to play more. The Ogre steps aside, letting us pass, as we say our thanks and goodbyes. He says back, "Thank you for playing. Come back again to play!" The Ogre is back in a good mood.

We enter through the stone archway onto a stage where the old man greets us. "Very well!" He says. "You have done very well. We will wait for the next contestant to arrive." While we wait, I look around at all the people sitting down to watch us in the last game. My eyes wander up to a large box where some of the royalty were watching us. It is at the top of the stadium for the best view. While a few of the royalty watch the beginning of the games, most or even all of them like watching the last game, so they sit in the selected box.

A few minutes later, a taller and older girl with short white hair, baby blue eyes, and white skin breathlessly staggers through the archway. She is the one who ran back to the starting line after running with her friends right up to the Ogre. She glares at us, and takes her place a few feet away from us. I remember always seeing her in town and I think her name is Snow.

The old man steps forward and speaks. “Very well done children! Now you will need to pick your horses out. You two first. Pick out one horse to share.” He indicates for us to choose. I look at the horses, and the neon yellow one stares me in the eyes. I look at Shimmer, and she is also looking at the yellow horse. I know it has picked us, so we automatically decide on the yellow one. It seems that this horse is made out of yellow lightning right from the heavens above. The light from the horse is almost blinding.

Snow takes the black horse, and she doesn’t seem very happy. In fact, she scowls, and tries to kick the horse. It moves its leg out of the way in time, and she ends up on the floor. Now, she’s as bright red as the red lightning bolts that periodically flash through the sky.

The old man speaks to us and says to put the stickers on the horse's shoulder, and we put the cinnamon colored stickers on. They stand out on the horse, and it looks good. I pat the horse, let it sniff me, scratch him, and I give him a hug. Shimmer does the same, and the horse looks energized. I look around the stadium, and see lots of people watching us.

The man says, "First, you will have a race on Lightning Birds. You will travel around the highest peak of the mountains, and get dropped off on your horses to travel around the track in the arena five times for you to win. The Lightning Birds will pick you up while in flight." Hc turned to us, pointed at Shimmer and I and said, "You two, hold hands and stay together. Now, let the last game begin!"

From our experience of watching previous games, and reading about them, Lightning Birds are giant birds. Their wingspan is nineteen feet long, and they weigh forty five pounds. The color of its feathers are speckled brown and white. They are very strong birds, able to carry more than their own weight. They nest and live in the highest mountain peaks surrounding the valley, and feed on fish from the sea and large mice from the low mountains. They are loyal to the royal family.

A loud crack of thunder sounded and large claws aiming for our waists appeared out of nowhere. I felt wind and looked down to find ourselves high above the meadow getting closer and closer, and higher and higher to the mountain tops. The claws throw us on top of the bird, and it squawks it's greetings. The Lightning Bird also tells us to hold on tight.

We grip a handful of feathers and lean forward, as it retracts it's legs and speeds up. The town below us gets smaller and smaller, and the whipping wind gets slightly colder as we gain altitude. Bolts of electricity shoot down as obstacles along the way and in the path. We maintain a steady course and no bolts of lightning hit us. As we turn around the back side of the mountain, a bolt of blue lightning strikes the Lightning Bird's left wing as we turn right. The light blinded us, and we all had to close our eyes.

A shriek emitted from the bird, and a sickening jolt filled my stomach. My eyes flew open, to see the valley floor. We were in a nosedive. I looked at Shimmer, and she turned her head to me. She had a determined face. I looked back at where we were headed in front of us just as we leveled off. The Lightning Bird recovered, and started a slight climb. The bolts of electric charged particles filled the sky. It was so beautiful. We turned onto the last leg of our course, and the bird cawed directions at us to adjust into the right positions. We said bye and thank you before being flung up, and caught between the Lightning Bird's strong claws.

I cannot see the other Lightning Bird right now, or Snow. I see clearly the bright yellow of our horse keeping pace with us as we come closer, and the claws bring us together and let us go directly onto the horse. It starts galloping faster immediately as soon as it feels our weight bear down on it. On the track and ahead of us, we see Snow. The horse tells us that she has just started her second lap.

We easily pass her, and she becomes furious. We maintain our steady pace, and she forces her horse into its fastest speed. She matches us, and then speeds forward ahead of us. We keep a steady pace behind her. We go two laps like this and a pink bolt of lightning randomly strikes the ground in the middle of the stadium. It is a pretty hue.

We turn onto our next leg, and we see the horse in front of us slow down from exhaustion. We pass them easily, and now we are speeding up to our fastest speed. Everything is a blur as we go easily around one lap and another. I catch a glimpse of something white and black on the course that we pass twice. We pass the finish line just as yellow lightning bolts surround the stadium. The crowd cheers in admiration.

We trot over to the old man on the platform smiling broadly. I can now see his eyes. They are a mix of all the colors. There's yellow, purple, orange, pink, blue, red, brown, and green surrounding his black pupils. He snaps, and two head wreaths appear on his arm along with a sash. They are golden yellow, shimmering and glowing. Shapes of lightning bolts, Shimmer and I, the horse, the Ogre, the lightning bolt figurines, and the Lightning Bird are intertwined.

Snow rides up, and jumps off of her horse, not looking the slightest bit happy at all. Her short white hair is slightly frazzled from the wind whipping it around. She looks as if she is about to say something. The old man holds up his hand to keep her silent, and speaks to the black horse. He thanks and dismisses it, before turning to the girl with white hair.

He says, "Snow, thank you for participating in the Lightning Horse Game. You should know now that you need to be kind and encouraging to your horse. You were participating in the opposite way. Your competing opponents were loving, supportive, kind, and encouraging. Thank you again. If you would like, you may leave, or stay." Snow nods her head, and has seemed to calm down. Then she walks back through the stone archway we first came through. The old man now turns to us.

In a loud voice, he turns to the audience, and shouts, "Ladies and Gentlemen, boys and girls, the winners of The Lightning Games, Lightning and Shimmer!" His arms are up, holding our hands up like heroes. His voice echoes off the walls, but not for long. The crowd cheers in excitement. The cheering is louder than the mightiest and loudest boom of thunder. As the crowd quiets down, he presents the wreaths to us and puts them on our heads each in turn. We each whisper our thanks, and he smiles. He adjusts the wreaths, and we turn to the crowd. The horse steps forward and bows its head to receive the sash. It neighs it's thanks, and also turns to the crowd. They roar with another round of clapping, cheering, and admiration even louder than the first. “This brings us to the conclusion of The Lightning Games.” He announces. “Thank you to all who participated. We will wait until the next game. Farewell!” In a flash of green lightning, he’s gone.

Our horse snorts, telling us to get on. We ride out of the arena, and trot through the meadow, through the streets, and to our home. We tell the horse to wait there as we run inside to get some water and apples, for the horse. We let the horse drink and eat. Soon, our proud parents arrive home. We make a bed in the shed for the horse, and store water and some apples in there. The horse nuzzles up to us each in turn, before settling in and quickly falling asleep for a short nap. Then he will have to return home to the castle. We eat some bread, cheese, lettuce, and sliced meat while we talk and laugh together. We don’t usually eat like this. This is a celebratory meal. We sleepily and thankfully go to bed. We all happily dream of horses, Lightning Birds, the Ogre, and the fun game itself.

In the morning, the sky is clear with no sign of any clouds, and the sun is warm on our backs. We excitedly run to the shed to find it empty, except for a glowing yellow paper, the same color of the horse. The black inked handwriting is neat and elegant cursive. In the bottom corner, is the stamp or seal of the eldest prince. We read the letter together. It states, "Dear Lightning and Shimmer, thank you for your hospitality and endurance throughout the Lightning Horse Game. I have to admit it was very fun competing with you both. It was also very pleasant meeting you and being your horse. I enjoyed your lively spirit and encouragement. My younger brother is the black horse, and to tell you a secret, we all do not know why his color is black. There cannot be black lightning. We hope that it is just a mistake or sign from the heavens above. I wish to someday meet you in person. I will send a note like this to you the day before I visit to give a notice in advance. Thank you again for your generosity. Yours truly, Prince Albert". The glowing letter is framed in our house for us to remember. Now, we wait for his visit, and the next Lightning Games.

The End.

How this book came to be.

This book started out as a dream. In fact, most of this book is my dream. My dream stopped right about where the "girl with white hair" came through the stone archway into the stadium. Right there, I started waking up, and my dream could not be continued. Multiple nights after that, I tried setting myself up to replicate the dream, but it wouldn't happen. With an amazing and invigorating unfinished dream, I decided I wanted to share it with others. I then wrote down the dream that I dreamt, and started from there. I constantly thought, "How would this next part go if I were dreaming?" It all worked out well, and now I am left with an ecstatic dreamlike story. I would have liked to know what would have happened if my dream had been continued, but that's how this book came to be.

About The Author

My name is Bella, and I am in eighth grade. I have two younger sisters, Ava and Elly, who I love to play with. I enjoy writing stories, going to the park, playing sports, biking, hiking, seeing and exploring new places, creating art, inventing, helping out, and learning new skills. I have also written and created a few other books with my sisters. They are Skip my School story and song book, ABC I Am Me - The Fruity Addition, The Animal Addition Adventure, and the Positive I Am book for all. We are also the Trio Travelers, NPS Kids, and Tyme to Dyne. Aside from that, we also create Shroomeez, magical mushroom friends. We all live in a lush green valley in Honolulu, Hawaii. So far, I think this is my best and most accomplishcd book that I've written. I will continue to write stories, and share them with everyone. Thank you for reading my story.

www.ingramcontent.com/pod-product-compliance
Ingram Content Group UK Ltd.
Pitfield, Milton Keynes, MK11 3LW, UK
UKHW021926190726
13853UKWH00002B/865